VIKING VIK

In the year 874, Vikings ruled the waves, sailing the seas in their powerful Longships. And in a small village called Snekkevik, Freya, Wulf and Vik were born. On the same day!

When Vik lost his parents in a great battle a year later, he was adopted by Freya and Wulf's family, who took him in as their own son.

But Vik and Wulf never did see eye to eye...

"I'M THE LEADER!"

FOR
KJELL OTTO

First published in 2008 by Orchard Books
First paperback publication in 2009

ORCHARD BOOKS
338 Euston Road, London NW1 3BH
Orchard Books Australia
Level 17/207 Kent St, Sydney, NSW 2000

ISBN 978 1 84616 720 1 (hardback)
ISBN 978 1 84616 728 7 (paperback)

Text and illustrations © Shoo Rayner 2008

The right of Shoo Rayner to be identified as the author and
illustrator of this work has been asserted by him in accordance with the
Copyright, Designs and Patents Act, 1988.

A CIP catalogue record for this book is available from the British Library.

1 3 5 7 9 10 8 6 4 2 (hardback)
1 3 5 7 9 10 8 6 4 2 (paperback)

Printed in Great Britain

Orchard Books is a division of Hachette Children's Books,
an Hachette Livre UK company.

www.hachettelivre.co.uk

Just then, Jarl Magnusson came striding down the jetty. "A Longship is no place for children," he boomed.

"Oh, Dad!" Freya fluttered her eyelashes. She knew how to get around her father – but it didn't work this time.

"Longships are definitely not for girls!" he told her firmly.

Vik longed to sail on a Longship. Just like his father, the sea flowed in Vik's blood.

"Will we ever get to sail on her?" he sighed.

Jarl Magnusson smiled, and spoke gently to Vik. "When you are strong enough and old enough to understand the dangerous ways of the ocean, then you can sail aboard a Longship."

Jarl Magnusson turned to his men and began shouting orders. "Come on, you slack-jawed jellyfish! Get this ship ready before the weather changes. It's time to put the *Dragon* through her paces."

The *Dragon* was brand-new. For the last few months, Vik had watched her being built on the shore at Snekkevik. The graceful ship had not yet been out of the fiord. It was time for her to be tested on the high seas.

FIORDS

During the ice ages, glaciers cut deep valleys into the rocky mountains in Scandanavia.

When the glaciers melted, the valleys were flooded by the sea and became "fiords".

Fiords are very deep and give excellent shelter for ocean-going ships.

"We could watch them sail from the skerries," Vik suggested.

"Good idea," said Wulf. "Let's go."

The three children and Vik's dog, Flek, ran all the way to the mouth of the fiord.

The skerries were a chain of small islands that reached out into the sea like a rocky necklace.

Flek splashed in the rock pools.
It was low tide, and the children
soon hopped out to the furthest
island, where they waited for the
Dragon to sail past.

"We're quite far out, aren't we?"
Freya's voice trembled slightly. "Are
you sure we're safe out here?"

"Not scared, are you?"
Wulf taunted.

"No…just
as long as we
can get back
safely."

It was a while before the
sleek vessel sailed into view.
"Hurray!" the children
cheered madly.

Jarl Magnusson stood at the prow. He waved his arms and called to them.

"What did he say?" Vik asked.

"Don't know," said Wulf. "I couldn't hear him."

"Never mind," said Vik, as he carried on cheering. "Go, *Dragon*, go!"

LONGSHIPS

Longships are sleek and deadly warships. They can sail across raging, stormy oceans, and glide up shallow rivers.

Vikings spend their summers sailing on Longships to raid distant villages and steal all their food and treasure.

The children strained
to see the last of the
Dragon as she sailed
over the grey horizon
and out onto the big,
wide ocean.

When they turned to go home, the three children had the shock of their lives. They had waited so long for the *Dragon* to sail past, they hadn't noticed that the tide had turned and the sea level had begun to rise.

Some of the little islands were already underwater!

"Quick! Let's go!" said Vik, leaping across a gap that swirled with foam and rushing water. "We can make it back to shore if we hurry."

It was quite a stretch to the
next island. Vik could just see
the gravelly rocks under the
lapping waves.

"It's not too
deep," Vik called.
"We can wade
across if we hold
hands and stick
together."

Just then, Flek barked.
Freya screamed and
pointed. A long black
fin cut through the
water nearby.

"Orca!" Wulf hissed.

More fins broke
the surface.

Something huge and dark rose
out of the water and rolled past the
tiny island. A cruel eye watched
them and a vicious mouth opened,
showing needle-sharp teeth.

They were surrounded by
orca – the fierce killer whales.
They were trapped!

"I don't think they eat people," said
Vik, trying to stay calm.

"Well, I don't want to be the first to
find out if you're wrong!" said Freya.

"What are we going to do?" It was
Wulf's turn to sound frightened.

Vik looked all around for a way out.
Could they get to the shore? Would the
orca eat them alive?

Their best chance was to get back
to the island from where they had
watched the *Dragon* sail. It was the
largest island with the highest land.
Maybe they could survive there until
the tide went out again.

Vik made up his mind. They needed to stay alive. They could worry about getting off the island later. "Follow me!" he ordered. "We need to get above the tide."

The children huddled together with Flek. The tide crept higher and higher up the side of the rocky island. Every few minutes a large wave lapped the rocks and sprayed them with foam.

"We're lucky it's not windy," Wulf said. "The waves would be much higher."

"I wish those horrid orca would go away," Freya whined. Her voice sounded weak and tired.

The orca had all the time in the world. Maybe they were waiting for the children to grow tired and slip into the water! Could things get any worse?

"What is that?" Vik stared at a huge, dark shape that was rolling towards them from the ocean. It was so large it blackened the sky. Vik remembered the god Thor, and his battle with Jormundgand, the World Serpent.

"Jormundgand!" Vik closed his eyes. The monster of the deep was coming to finish them off!

THOR AND JORMUNDGAND

Jormundgand is the son of the god Loki. He is so big that he can wrap his body around the Earth and grasp his tail in his mouth.

Legend says that at the end of the world Thor will kill the beast, but not before Jormundgand poisons Thor with his terrifying teeth.

The wall of darkness rolled over them like a cold, wet blanket.

A strange, ghostly, rhythmic sound echoed through the foggy mist. Vik listened hard.

"Jormundgand!" he whispered again.
"It's coming to get us!"

"I want my dad!" Freya whimpered.

The sound came closer and closer.
Flek barked at the invisible monster.

Suddenly, out of the gloom, the serpent's head towered above them.

The children screamed, and the sound stopped. A familiar voice called through the gloom. "Who's there?"

"It's me, Vik Haraldson!" Vik yelled.

The serpent edged closer.
Vik opened his eyes. It wasn't
a serpent...it was a dragon.
In fact it was the *Dragon*!

Jarl Magnusson's huge face appeared through the mist. "Vik!" he growled. "I told you children to get back to the shore!"

Then his face softened into a smile.
"But it's lucky for us that you got stuck
out here. We would have crashed into
the rocks if we hadn't heard Flek," he
explained. "We were lost in the fog. You
may well have saved the *Dragon*."

Flek wagged
his tail. He knew
he had done well.

The men began rowing again and the *Dragon* cut through the silent water. Freya told her father all about the orca and the rising tide.

"Well, that's one way to get a ride on a Longship," he laughed when she had finished.

He turned to the boys.
"You two have certainly
learnt something about
the dangerous ways of the
ocean today."

"Yes, sir." The boys hung their heads. They expected Jarl Magnusson to tell them off for getting into a mess.

He smiled. "Perhaps it's time to let one of you take a longer trip on the *Dragon*."

The two boys eyed each other and smiled. Finally each had a chance to sail properly on a Longship. But which one would it be?

"I'm the strongest!" Wulf said, smirking.

Jarl Magnusson's eyes twinkled. "Let's wait until next summer."

Vik said nothing. He stood at the prow of the *Dragon* and felt her moving under his feet.

A competition had begun between him and Wulf. Vik was determined to show Jarl Magnusson that he would be a worthy winner!

SHOO RAYNER

Viking Vik and the Wolves	978 1 84616 725 6
Viking Vik and the Big Fight	978 1 84616 731 7
Viking Vik and the Chariot Race	978 1 84616 730 0
Viking Vik and the Trolls	978 1 84616 724 9
Viking Vik and the Bug House	978 1 84616 726 3
Viking Vik and the Lucky Stone	978 1 84616 727 0
Viking Vik and the Longship	978 1 84616 728 7
Viking Vik and the Secret Shield	978 1 84616 729 4

All priced at £3.99

The Viking Vik stories are available from all good bookshops,
or can be ordered direct from the publisher:
Orchard Books, PO BOX 29, Douglas IM99 1BQ
Credit card orders please telephone 01624 836000
or fax 01624 837033 or visit our internet site: www.orchardbooks.co.uk
or e-mail: bookshop@enterprise.net for details.

To order please quote title, author and ISBN
and your full name and address.
Cheques and postal orders should be made payable to 'Bookpost plc.'
Postage and packing is FREE within the UK
(overseas customers should add £2.00 per book).

Prices and availability are subject to change.